Why Does Izzy Cover Her Ears?

Why Does Izzy Cover Her Ears?

Dealing with Sensory Overload

Written and Illustrated by
Jennifer Veenendall

APC
Autism Asperger Publishing Co.
P.O. Box 23173
Shawnee Mission, Kansas 66283-0173
www.asperger.net

©2009 Autism Asperger Publishing Company
P.O. Box 23173
Shawnee Mission, Kansas 66283-0173
www.asperger.net

Publisher's Cataloging-in-Publication

Veenendall, Jennifer.
    Why does Izzy cover her ears? : dealing with sensory overload /
written and illustrated by Jennifer Veenendall. -- 1st ed. -- Shawnee
Mission, Kan. : Autism Asperger Pub. Co., c2009.

        p. ; cm.
        ISBN: 978-1-934575-46-8
        LCCN: 2009924242
        Includes discussion questions and recommended resources.
        Audience: Ages 5-10.
        Summary: Illustrated children's book dealing with the
challenges at home and at school of sensory overload--symptoms
and tools for mitigating them and enabling children to function and
learn more successfully.

    1. Sensory integration dysfunction in children. 2. Children with
disabilities--Education. 3. Children with disabilities--Juvenile fiction.
4. [People with disabilities--Education. 5. People with disabilities--
Fiction. 6. Senses and sensation--Fiction.] I. Title. II. Title: Dealing
with sensory overload.

RJ496.S44 V449 2009
618.92/85883--dc22   0903

This book is designed in CG Benguiat Frisky.

Printed in the United States of America.

To all the "Izzys" who have helped me understand this disorder without even knowing it.

To my family. I'm deeply thankful for your support of my new adventures.

Acknowledgments

I would like to thank Mary Sue Williams and Shelly Shellenberger for their *How Does Your Engine Run? Alert Program for Self-Regulation.* They have provided occupational therapists, teachers, and families with a brilliant tool to help children with sensory modulation difficulties feel more understood, confident, and more in control of their success at home and at school. This book is intended to be used with such a program to help all elementary students understand the basic concepts of sensory modulation and the tools that all of us can use to "tune our engines," when necessary.

I would also like to thank Dr. Lucy Miller for her dedication to children with sensory processing needs and her commitment to help us all learn more about this disorder and its underlying causes through her ongoing research.

Jennifer Veenendall

Hi. My name is Izzy. I started first grade 32 days ago. I hate to tell you, but it has not been as great as my kindergarten teacher said it would be.

I cried a lot of the first 20 days or so. And I spent a lot of time looking for a safe place to get away from all the craziness that was going on.

When everything became too much for me, I hid under the computer table.

Center time was one of the things I hated the most. They should call it something else, like "crazy loud time." Grace was always in my group; we sat at the blue table with Ben. Grace could draw trees that don't look like lollipops. Her trees look like real trees. And she can make a rhyme with any word you say. But she has a voice that hurts my ears. It makes my insides rattle. I felt like pushing her away from my ears to make her stop talking "into" me when she was playing her rhyming game.

But I know that hands are not for hitting, so instead I usually cried and covered my ears. I couldn't help it. It hurt! The kids called me a baby. But I'm not a baby. Noisy places make me feel frustrated.

I also threw a lot of tantrums to get out of class and spend some time in Mr. Otterson's office. He's our principal. His office is quiet, and there is a beanbag chair in there that I love to sit in. I feel a lot more relaxed there.

Another thing that was hard about first grade in the beginning was that there are more kids in my class than last year. More kids to bump into me if they forget their line basics and more kids to step on my shoelaces when I'm trying to put my backpack in my locker in the morning.

When kids bumped into me, I used to think they were being bullies and trying to pick on me. My teacher would say, "Izzy, that was an accident. Alexander didn't mean to bump into you." I still wanted to belt him. I felt like I was going to blow into pieces.

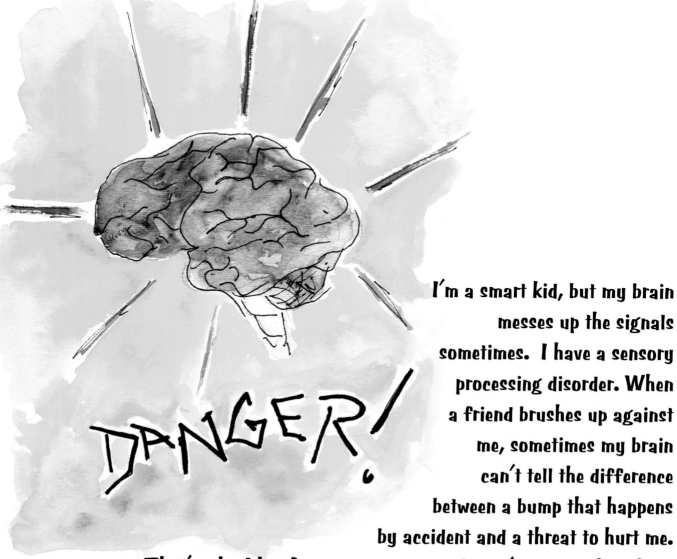

DANGER!

I'm a smart kid, but my brain messes up the signals sometimes. I have a sensory processing disorder. When a friend brushes up against me, sometimes my brain can't tell the difference between a bump that happens by accident and a threat to hurt me. That's why I hit Alexander one time. I didn't mean to hurt him, but my brain thought I was in danger, so I defended myself by hitting.

My mom and dad, my teachers, and an occupational therapist have been trying to help me. The occupational therapist at my school helps kids learn to listen to their bodies and find ways to feel calmer and ready to learn. She's been helping me figure out the things that make me feel uncomfortable and angry at school. By working with her, I found out that I am not a mean kid or a crybaby, like some of the other kids said.

17

My brain also
tells me that
sounds are
louder than
they really are.
At home, I hate
the noise from the
hairdryer and the vacuum cleaner.
I used to cover my ears and cry when my mom turned them on. I have learned
that it's a little better if she warns me before she turns them on. Sometimes I
put my headphones on to block out the noise. That works, too.

Mom says the vacuum makes me irritable. When I'm irritable, I might slam the door
to my room, or I might yell at my little sister. I'm pretty sure "irritable" means
"crabby."

You know what else? Having too many things to look at really annoys me. My teacher is very proud of all the great artwork we do, but when she hangs everything we make from the ceiling, it's too much for me to look at. I have a hard time focusing on her calendar time when there are 26 giant construction paper apples floating around in the air. I also don't like the lights in our classroom. They are too bright and make it hard to think.

My teacher has made some changes here at school to help me. Things are much better. Now, I'm sitting with a different group of kids at the yellow table by Mrs. Malone's desk. I like Grace lots more from a distance because her voice doesn't hurt my ears.

For other noises that used to bother me, I wear earplugs if I need them. I can use them in the lunchroom and during gym class. These are especially noisy places at school. When I can tune out hurtful noises, I can concentrate on the more important things like getting my work done, eating lunch, and playing games in gym class, instead of worrying about how loud it is around me.

My locker is on the end now, so I have more space. I don't get bumped into as much, and I don't feel as mad. Mrs. Malone says I have a bigger space bubble. My friends know about my bubble, and they try not to pop it.

But even with these changes, things can still get to be too much for me at school. When that happens, I spend some time in the motor room, swinging, crashing, and jumping. The motor room is like a small gym, with swings and jumpy things. I also play games called "Izzy Taco" and "Steamroller."

When I play Izzy Taco, I pretend a big heavy mat is a taco shell, and I roll up inside with pillows and beanbags that I pretend are lettuce, cheese, and sour cream. When I play Steamroller, I lie down on my tummy and get flattened by a big ball. These games help me relax my body, so I feel calmer when I go back to class and can concentrate on my work and be around the other kids.

I also use some tools at school to help me feel calm so I can learn better. I use a heavy blanket on my lap during morning meeting.

Sometimes I squeeze a fidget. My favorite is a yellow, squishy ball. Mrs. Malone calls it a hand tool.

I still have some hard days, but my tools are helping me feel calmer and I am able to focus better on the important things in school. My teachers understand me better.

When we are writing in our journals, my teacher plays classical music. These kinds of sounds make me feel more organized and help me concentrate.

The changes Mrs. Malone made to our classroom make me feel lots better. Mrs. Malone took down some of our artwork in the room. She also took down some of her other decorations and got some storage bins where she put lots of learning stuff that used to sit on the counters. Mrs. Malone doesn't turn the fluorescent lights on as much any more. There's a lamp in our room instead, and sometimes she lets a sunny day light our room. She says all the kids seem more focused now. I guess some things that bother me bother other kids, too. Never thought of that before. There's even a twelve-year-old kid down the street, Brad, who has the same kind of problems.

27

Being at home is a lot easier because there is not as much commotion as there is at school. But when I do start feeling irritable at home, there are things I can do there, too.

I can cool off in my room when things get to be too much. I like it there. I turn the lights down and sit in my beanbag chair under my heavy blanket. I feel my breathing slow down and soon I feel happier again. The crabbiness disappears.

I think first grade is going to be O.K. I have lots of friends. My mom and
dad think my reading rocks. They are so proud of me.

Sensory Processing and Sensory Modulation Disorders

In her book *The Out-of-Sync Child* (2005), Carol Stock Kranowitz describes sensory processing disorder as "the inability to use information received through the senses in order to function smoothly in daily life" (p. 9). There are different types of sensory processing disorders.

Izzy in this book is an example of somebody who has difficulties with a type of sensory processing disorder called sensory modulation. That is, her nervous system overresponds to many forms of sensory input. This is sometimes referred to as "sensory defensiveness." Dr. Lucy Jane Miller describes sensory overresponsivity in her book *Sensational Kids* (2006). According to Miller, children with this subtype of sensory processing disorder react to sensory input with more intensity and more quickly, and/or for a longer period of time than their typical peers.

Sensations that most children ignore can provoke a feeling of threat in a child with sensory overresponsivity, who therefore reacts in unexpected ways. Because various forms of sensory input easily overstimulate these children, they have a difficult time with transitions, for example. By avoiding change, they are able to create comfort for themselves. They may become aggressive, or they may become very withdrawn when they feel uncomfortable with sensations (Miller, 2006). As illustrated, Izzy's nervous system overreacts to noise, too much visual input, and unexpected bumps or tactile input. Her behavioral response is to withdraw or melt down, and sometimes become aggressive.

With the help of her teachers, parents, and an occupational therapist, Izzy has learned to use sensorimotor strategies to help herself self-regulate – that is, deal with constantly feeling like there is too much sensation. She uses a variety of tools and materials that provide her nervous system with input with calming qualities. For example, she uses a weighted blanket, ear protection, and a hand-held fidget to squeeze. Her family and teachers have also made accommodations for her in the classroom and at home to ensure that she does not feel overstimulated by various types of input such as unexpected touch, loud sounds, and distracting or aversive visual input. The combination of tools, strategies, and accommodations has resulted in fewer tears and less aggression. Izzy is more available for learning and positive social opportunities. She is a more confident first grader.

Suggested Discussion Questions Following Reading the Book with a Child or a Group of Children

1. **Do you think Izzy was trying to be naughty or get other kids and her teacher to pay more attention to her by throwing tantrums and hiding under tables?** (Izzy was trying to be good, but she was having a hard time dealing with a lot of things at school that made her feel nervous and uncomfortable.)

2. **What kinds of things make Izzy feel scared, angry, or uncomfortable?** (She is sensitive to sounds, like loud voices and vacuum cleaners. She also is sensitive to accidental bumps and touches.)

3. **What are some of the changes Izzy's teacher made to help Izzy feel more comfortable at school so she could make friends easier and focus on learning?** (She moved her to a quieter spot in the classroom, moved her locker to the end of the hall, so she didn't get bumped as much, and she explained to the other students that Izzy needed a bigger space bubble. She also removed some of the extra things to look at in the classroom.)

4. **What are some tools that Izzy used to help her feel calmer so she could focus on the important things at school?** (ear protectors/plugs, weighted blanket, fidgets, and music)

5. **Izzy uses tools to help her feel calm and ready to learn. Think about other types of tools people might use to help them be more successful.**
   - What tool would a person use if he could not see as well as others? (glasses)
   - What would a person use if she could not hear as well as others? (hearing aid)
   - What would a student use if her muscles work differently and she has a hard time walking? (walker or wheelchair)

Recommended Resources for Teachers and Parents

Aquilla, P., Sutton, S., & Yack, E. (2002). *Building bridges through sensory integration*. Las Vegas, NV: Sensory Resources.

Aspy, R., & Grossman, B. G. (2008). *The Ziggurat Model: A framework for designing comprehensive interventions for individuals with high-functioning autism and Asperger Syndrome*. Shawnee Mission, KS: Autism Asperger Publishing Company.

Biel, L., & Peske, N. K. (2005). *Raising a sensory smart child*. New York: Penguin Books.

Brack, J. (2004). *Learn to move, move to learn: Sensorimotor early childhood activity themes*. Shawnee Mission, KS: Autism Asperger Publishing Company.

Brack, J. (2009). *Learn to move, moving up: Sensorimotor elementary-school activity themes*. Shawnee Mission, KS: Autism Asperger Publishing Company.

Brack, J. (2005). *Sensory processing disorder: Simulations & solutions for parents, teachers and therapists*. (DVD). Shawnee Mission, KS: Autism Asperger Publishing Company.

Davalos, S. R. (2000). *Making sense of art: Sensory-based activities for children with autism, Asperger Syndrome, and other pervasive developmental disorders*. Shawnee Mission, KS: Autism Asperger Publishing Company.

Fuge, G., & Berry, R. (2004). *Pathways to play! Combining sensory integration and integrated play groups*. Shawnee Mission, KS: Autism Asperger Publishing Company.

Godwin Emmans, P., & McEndry Anderson, L. (2005). *Understanding sensory dysfunction: Learning, development and sensory dysfunction in autism spectrum disorders, ADHD, learning disabilities and bipolar disorder*. London, Philadelphia: Jessica Kingsley Publishers.

Henry, D. A. (2000). *Tool chest: For teachers, parents, and students: A handbook to facilitate self-regulation*. Glendale, AZ: Henry Occupational Therapy Service, Inc.

Kerstein, L. H. (2008). *My sensory book: Working together to explore sensory issues and the big feelings they can cause – A workbook for parents, professionals, and children.* Shawnee Mission, KS: Autism Asperger Publishing Company.

Koomar, J., Kranowitz, C., Szkut, S., Balzer-Martin, L., Haber, E., & Sava, D. (2004). *Answers to questions teachers ask about sensory integration.* Las Vegas, NV: Sensory Resources LLC.

Kranowitz, C. (1995). *101 activities for kids in tight spaces.* New York: St. Martin's.

Kranowitz, C. (2005). *The out-of-sync child: Recognizing and coping with sensory processing disorder, 2nd edition.* New York: Perigee Books.

Kranowitz, C. (2006). *The out-out-sync child has fun: Activities for kids with sensory processing disorder, 2nd edition.* New York: Perigee Books.

Miller, L. J. (2006). *Sensational kids.* New York: G. P. Putnam's Sons.

Myles, B. S., Cook, K. T., Miller, N. E., Rinner, L., & Robbins, L. A. (2000). *Asperger syndrome and sensory issues: Practical solutions for making sense of the world.* Shawnee Mission, KS: Autism Asperger Publishing Company.

Sangirardi Ganz, J. (2005). *Including SI for parents: Sensory integration strategies at home and school.* Prospect, CT: Biographical Publishing Company.

Shellenberger, S., & Williams, M. S. (1994). *An introduction to how does your engine run?: The alert program for self-regulation.* Albuquerque, NM: Therapy Works, Inc.

Shellenberger, S., & Williams, M. S. (1996). *How does your engine run?: A leader's guide to the alert program for self-regulation.* Albuquerque, NM: TherapyWorks, Inc.

Shellenberger, S., & Williams, M. S. (2001). *Take five! Staying alert at home and school.* Albuquerque, NM: Therapy Works, Inc.

Useful Websites

1. www.alertprogram.com
   This is the Alert Program (Shellenberger & Williams) website. It describes the program, offers products, conference information, articles, and other resources related to the Alert Program.

2. www.ateachabout.com
   This is the Henry Occupational Therapy Services, Inc. site. It includes a variety of products useful to parents, teachers, and students written by Diana A. Henry, such as books and DVDs. Sensory products such as fidgets, weighted materials, and CDs can be ordered through a link on this site. It also provides information about workshops, articles, and other resources related to sensory processing disorders.

3. www.SensoryResources.com
   The Sensory Resources website offers products such as books, CDs, videos, and DVDs as well as information on workshops and conferences.

4. www.sensorysmarts.com
   This is the website by the authors of *Raising a Sensory Smart Child* (Biel & Peske, 2005). It includes several useful sections with tips and resources for parents of children with sensory processing disorders.

5. www.sensorystories.com
   This website links users to a web application of illustrated sensory e-stories for children with overresponsive sensory modulation.

6. www.SIFocus.com
   This is the website for *S.I. Focus*, the international magazine dedicated to improving sensory integration.

7. www.SPDconnection.com
   This is the website for Jenny's Kids Inc. founded by Jenny Clark Brack, OTR/L, BCP. The site is dedicated to providing sensory integration solutions for parents, teachers, and therapists. It lists activities, products, and services.

8. www.SPDfoundation.net
   This is the website for The Sensory Processing Disorder Foundation. It is a project of the KID foundation, a nonprofit organization that focuses on research, education, and advocacy related to sensory processing disorders.

Recommended Children's Books

Berns, J. M., Chara, C. P., Chara, K. A., & Chara, P. J. (2004). *Sensory smarts: A book for kids with ADHD or autism spectrum disorders struggling with sensory integration problems.* London; Philadelphia: Jessica Kingsley Publishers.

Gagnon, E., & Myles, B. S. (1999). *This is Asperger Syndrome.* Shawnee Mission, KS: Autism Asperger Publishing Company.

Keating Velasco, J. (2007). *A is for autism, F is for friend; A kid's book on making friends with a child who has autism.* Shawnee Mission, KS: Autism Asperger Publishing Company.

Keating Velasco, J. (2007). *In his shoes: A short journey through autism.* Shawnee Mission, KS: Autism Asperger Publishing Company.

Kerstein, L. H. (2008). *My sensory book: Working together to explore sensory issues and the big feelings they can cause – A workbook for parents, professionals, and children.* Shawnee Mission, KS: Autism Asperger Publishing Company.

Kranowitz, C. (2004). *The Goodenoughs get in sync: An introduction to sensory processing disorder.* Las Vegas, NV: Sensory Resources.

Larson, E. M. (2006). *I am utterly unique – Celebrating the strengths of children with Asperger Syndrome and high-functioning autism.* Shawnee Mission, KS: Autism Asperger Publishing Company.

Larson, E. M. (2007). *The kaleidoscope kid – Focusing on the strengths and children with Asperger Syndrome and high-functioning autism.* Shawnee Mission, KS: Autism Asperger Publishing Company.

Larson, E. M. (2008). *Chameleon kid – Controlling meltdown before he controls you.* Shawnee Mission, KS: Autism Asperger Publishing Company.

Lowell, J., & Tuchel, T. (2005). *My best friend Will.* Shawnee Mission, KS: Autism Asperger Publishing Company.

Murrell, D. (2004). *Oliver Onion – The onion who learns to accept and be himself.* Shawnee Mission, KS: Autism Asperger Publishing Company.

Peralta, S. (2002). *All about my brother.* Shawnee Mission, KS: Autism Asperger Publishing Company.

Renke, L. (2005). *I like birthdays ... it's the parties I'm not sure about.* Las Vegas, NV: Sensory Resources.

Veenendall, J. (2008). *Arnie and his school tools: Simple sensory solutions that build success.* Shawnee Mission, KS: Autism Asperger Publisher Company.

APC

Autism Asperger Publishing Co.
P.O. Box 23173
Shawnee Mission, Kansas 66283-0173
www.asperger.net • 913-897-1004